STAIRCASE

by David Fenske

Published 2011

Contact: info@staircasethemovie.com
Website: www.staircasethemovie.com

Cover Artist: Gary Fenske - www.fenskeart.com
Editors: Judy Peterson & Sher Kunz

The Author

David Fenske has the unusual talent of remembering very complicated dreams.

This novel blends together two of his dreams. Staircase and Riveocea were consecutive story dreams that haunted him. They kept reoccurring and the story built after each restless night. Waking up in the middle of the night, he finally wrote down the complete sequence until the recurring dreams stopped.

With bizarre twist and turns, the mystery of the Staircase plays with our mind and takes us into his deepest psyche. By the end many will read Staircase again just to pick up on missed clues.

Note from the author

Readers seem to interpret Staircase on a very personal level. I find satisfaction when my writings inspire the heart.

Dreams come from our subconscious. They reveal our innermost fears or joys and give insight into ones very being. What this book tells about me, I don't know. Analyze it. Break it down. Tear it apart. Then, give me your interpretation.

You can let me know what you think by joining my Facebook page called 'Staircase, The Movie'.

Answer for me the question: **"What is the Staircase?"**

Portal 1

"Of all the possibilities in the Multiverse I find static in the Harmonics level to be the most unfathomable."

- Excerpt from the lost papers of N.T. -

Girls, Girls, Girls

It was my last door. An end to a long week of cold calling. How I hate my job.

Can't wait to have a final nightcap and lay my head on a pillow. Thank god my hotel is not far from here.

Aside from my mood, it's a pleasant evening. Not too warm. Seems to be a perfect summer's night. A short walk through the streets of New York should find me a cozy little bar somewhere. I just need to relax. It should have been an easy task, but I just can't find the right atmosphere. Some are too stuffy, and others smell of old booze.

After a long day I get a dark attitude. Just hard to settle down and get the knot out of my stomach. Maybe I think too much.

Then again, my wife just served me divorce papers, living out of a suitcase, moving from hotel to hotel, and never quite making my sales goals, takes its toll.

Selling things to people who don't want to buy my

products puts me in a slow simmering rage. Why do I stick with this job?

Huh, that's weird; the street lamps seem darker than normal. Maybe just my disposition.

A small smile crosses my face.

Across the street, a slightly tilted red neon sign flickers. The way the last two letters flash on and off remind me of the old horror flicks.

It reads, "Girls, Girls, G__s".

"Why not, maybe this will cheer me up."

As I approach the door a feeling of déjà vu comes over me; even a little chill. It all seems too strangely familiar, even comfortable. The windows are painted shut. Even the paint on the door looks original. After years of weathering; I scratch a few flakes off.

The red, warm light from inside invites me in. So odd. I know I have never been here. Yet, it feels like I am going to my old hangout back home. I almost expect to see some old friends inside.

Turning the doorknob, the door swings like it has a mind of its own.

"Ha," I exclaim, "How ironic."

A trail worn in the old wood floor by years of traffic leads directly to my seat at the bar like it was waiting for me. The sign outside must have been a relic because there were no dancing girls inside. No matter.

"In my line of work I would call this a setup."

Actually, this is just what I am looking for. I spin the bar stool before sitting down. Somehow, I knew it would squeak.

At a back table in a dimly-lit corner, two young men are flirting with a couple of scantily clothed women. Oh, to be young again.

As I put my feet on top of the brass foot rest, the bartender slowly makes his way down the long bar to clear the empty beer glasses in front of me.

His reflection from the mirror behind the bar seems to blur for a second. Made me take a quick breath.

Looking in the mirror, I comb my hair. Losing a little on top, the rest of my hair is turning grey. At least it is hair. Actually, it doesn't look that bad against my new tan.

The walking I do on my job usually keeps me in shape. But, I could use a little work out.

My age is starting to show. If only I had more time. There are so many things I could do over. If only I had more time.

The bartender seems to be intentionally taking his time to wait on me. He is asking every patron he passes whether they need another drink.

I am in no hurry. Where do I have to go?

This feels so much like home. Why is that?

Finally he reaches me and says, "They call me Joe. Sorry for the delay. Friday night at 2:00am we usually get a lot of lost souls looking for a good time. What can I get you?"

"A dry martini, shaken not stirred," I snapped.

Something is off. Why was I so brusque? This job must be wearing me down. Faking smiles trying to make a sale to people who could care less. Sitting here, I don't feel the need to pretend.

Not everything about my old hangout was great. Maybe that would explain my foul attitude. I wonder why I would remember that now.

Must be the harsh looks from the guys in the corner and the bartender. They don't seem to like me here either. It feels way too familiar.

Maybe I should just go back to the hotel and get some sleep. As they say, tomorrow is another day. No better than today or yesterday, it still will be another day. Who knows? Life can be so mundane that it makes you want to scream.

I raise my hand to get the attention of the bartender. Out of the corner of my eye I spot movement in the shadows. I see a woman with blonde flowing hair that stretches to the middle of her back. It barely covers the V slit of her red dress. It did little to disguise her slim build with breasts to match her perfect face.

How could I have missed her? With my history what difference does it make?

As I was about to leave, she slowly lifts her head and looks directly into my eyes. I couldn't move. She could melt a candle from across the room. My heart skips when she starts to walk in my direction. Her confident stride tops off my assessment of her. Irrational as it seems, I want her.

She came close enough for me to feel her breath on my face. I think she was speaking. Her lips seem to be moving but I can't hear her. I am totally mesmerized.

Her lips stop moving and a slight, caring smile crosses her face. Lifting her hand, she gently touches my cheek and I smile. I slowly wake from my trance. We were like music with harmony from a song I had never heard before.

Even her voice is angelic. A melody echoes in my head as she spoke. "My name is Niki; you look like you need some company." I have heard that line often from "ladies of the night". Somehow I know this is different.

Collecting my thoughts, I start to speak, but her finger gently touches my lips. How wise not to spoil the moment. I realized how easily I could fall in love with this stranger.

Fearing disappointment, I look down at the bar, lift my drink and say, "You are very kind but you don't have to bother."

Niki smiles again and I melt. "No bother at all. I really want to."

With my silence I try to mentally push her away. I should leave.

But it is as if she knows me better than I know myself. This woman really is different. My thoughts of leaving slowly disappear as she erases my fears.

I start with small talk. With just a few well chosen words she has me confessing parts of my life that I have never discussed with anyone. My job, my home and family, even my divorce. Everything that I tried so hard to forget came out. I am not sure if she was feigning interest, but she seems to really care.

Time seems not to exist. We talked. I am not sure for how long. Suddenly I realize something is different. I feel good. I had carried my burdens alone for so many years, only now did I sense relief.

As I take a deep breath I realize that I know nothing about her. My mind flooded with questions.

Who is she?

What is it about this place?

Did destiny bring me here?

I have no idea where to start; there is so much I want to know. Collecting my thoughts, my first question to her is, "Who is the real Niki?"

Odd question I know, but it seems appropriate.

Her eyes open wide. A look of horror distorts her perfect face. Her hands fly up to cover her mouth as she starts to scream.

I feel a searing pain in my back. Unable to breathe I twist around.

A tall man in a dark hooded jacket holding a bloodied knife stands behind me. People are screaming and running in all directions. I slowly slip off the stool to the hardwood floor.

It is a strange feeling. Lying calmly on the floor, feeling blood pump in my neck. Peaceful in a way. The throbbing in my back seems to be going away. The scrambling feet turns into a blur.

Closing my eyes I feel Niki's fingers running through my hair.

Listening to my slowing heartbeat, a peace envelops me. A ringing in my ear. So pure. Like dew drops falling on crystals. Like the sweet sound of harmony. Somehow, it makes me feel complete.

I whisper, "Can you hear that?"

She smiles and slowly fades from view.

I'm going to miss Niki.

Staircase

Walking slowly, not wanting to open my eyes. I know where I am. By the absence of smell I can tell I am no longer in the bar. I have been here too many times.

How I wish this was just a dream, but this is reality. I call it the Staircase.

A massive crowd pushes me along a path about 100 feet wide. A sea of bobbing heads walking up a staircase with no steps. Just a never ending uphill ramp.

Walls on each side prevent us from wandering away. Impossible to go against the traffic, everyone walks in the same direction. At the same slow pace, we methodically move without emotion. Like a nightmare that never ends, we have no choice. We push on.

Doors randomly appear on each wall but no one enters them. So many people here that there is not even enough room to fall down. Still, unless a door calls us, there is no motivation to leave.

Where does the staircase lead? Maybe nowhere. Seems to go on forever.

Looking down, I open my eyes. I know I am walking but I can barely see my feet move. No one talks so I retreat to my inner thoughts.

Reflecting on my encounter with Niki; why did we have such a short time together? It's moments like those that keep me going year after year.

Eventually, I gather the courage to look up. I see wall-to-wall heads. There is an advantage to being slightly taller than most of the people. At least I can see where I am going, though that is a small favor.

The colorless walkway curves slightly to the left. Each step feels as if we are walking up a huge spiral driveway; an uphill road that goes on forever.

Reminds me of an airport parking garage where I parked my car just before the structure collapsed. Wonder if my car made it through. I know I didn't.

Oh well, can't find that door again anyway. Don't remember how many doors ago that was. Time has no meaning here.

A few dim lights flicker against the dingy grey walls. They should be replaced soon but they never are, not in here. Everything stays the same. That is just the way it is. The dark walls are colorless. The only hints of color come from the occasional door that appears on our path.

Yellow flickering lights illuminate each doorway. Barely readable signs above each door let me know what is behind the door.

For some reason I have never seen any one else go through the doors. No one. I guess they don't call to the others like they do to me.

I recognize some of the signs. Places like San Francisco, Hilton Hotel, Riveocea, Federal Building, and the Twin Towers all give me a feeling of foreboding, so I stay away.

What can be worse than these doldrums? Enter a door that repels you and you may find out. Behind the door you forget about the Staircase. Who knows who you will be or what you will look like when you enter an unknown door.

A few doors are named after occupations, but I don't enter. Doors with signs above them like Fireman, Police, Cook and so on; those doors never beckon me, so I stay on the path.

None of it means anything to me so I just keeping walking; keeping up with the rest of the zombies.

Hours, maybe even days. Time is irrelevant. Does the stairway ever end?

Then ahead, I see it….a small sign above one of the doors. Surprised I didn't miss it. Warmth envelopes me. Finally, I can feel again.

It is irresistible. I can feel myself coming alive.

The sign reads, "Girls, Girls, G_ls".

THAT'S IT!

Could I have a second chance?

Don't think I have ever seen the same door twice. Odd. Very odd. Even here.

I push myself through the crowd like a crazy man. Shoving and jumping. Desperate. I need to get to that door!

After several bumps and bruises from pushing my way though the catatonic walkers, I make it to the door. Even if Niki is not there, I will be relieved just to feel something again.

The door is old. I scratch off some weathered paint flakes. A soft red light from a crack under the door lites up my shoes. My anticipation rises.

This is where I met Niki.

I take a deep breath to muster up some nerve. My hand shakes as I turn the cold brass knob. The door slowly swings open without even the slightest push.

Portal 2

"Color, what a wonderful illusion. Our brain is wired to see the illusion of color. We interpret waves from the spectrum into marvelous combinations of red, green and blue. And now, my new sight sees the colors of the Harmonic spectrum. How do you explain color to the blind?"

- Excerpt from the lost papers of N.T. -

Rewind

There he is, Joe the bartender, at the other end of the bar, inattentive as usual. Behind him, his reflection in the mirror stutters again. Oddities seem to be the nature of this place.

The large round clock on the wood panel wall above him shows the time as "Saturday 2am". My God! I'm early. Niki hasn't met me yet. Maybe I can get it right this time.

Spotting Niki across the room, I think to myself, "I'll be ready this time."

The worn trail in the old wood floor leads to my barstool. Walking to the stool, I give it a spin. Feeling elated, I hear it squeak.

Carefully recalling my last meeting here, I sit down, knowing it will be a while before I get waited on. I push the empty glasses aside. Somehow even the smell of stale beer is exciting.

Though I seem to be enjoying this, the bartender takes an unusually long time to wait on me.

When he finally makes it to me, I speak first. "Hi Joe. How

about a martini? And while you are at it, I'd like to buy Niki a glass of her favorite."

Frowning, he shakes his head as he walks away. Did he remember me? What is it about this place?

I watch in the mirror behind. At the bar Niki and Joe have a long discussion. Seems a little heated.

Finally he returns, and pours two drinks. Setting them down in front of me, he walks away in disgust.

What did I do?

Niki walks toward me with a big smile. I thought I saw a glint of recognition in her smile but we haven't met yet so I know it was just my anticipation.

God it's good to see her.

As she comes closer, she touched her glass to mine and asks, "Do I know you?"

Of course she doesn't. At least not yet.

A simple and honest answer would be best. "No, not yet," I answer with a reassuring smile. She sits down beside me.

The way the corner of her mouth curls as she starts to smile is infectious. Almost like letting you know she knew something you didn't. Her smile said, "Me too."

The conversation starts easily. This time I want to know about her.

Starting with small talk, I quickly get deeper into her head.

18

I ask questions about her life, her childhood, hobbies, even her traumas. She is so open. It is refreshing. She answers everything.

Out of the corner of my eye I see the shadow--a dark grey jacket sneaking behind me. This time I am ready.

Just as he is about to strike, I reach around to grab his knife. I twist and barely dodge the blade. It is just enough to keep from getting stabbed in the back.

I grab his hand and spin. He loses his grip on the knife and it spins on the floor. Grabbing the knife off the floor, I jump on top of him. With my hands on the hilt, his knife is at the ready.

I pause for a second. I've never killed anyone.

The front door to the bar swings open. Two cops run in, guns in hand. One yells, "freeze!"

At exactly the same moment, the second cop fires. It is a perfect shot, right through the heart.

On the floor again, feeling the blood pump in my neck. I don't blame them. After all, I was the only man with a knife.

I hear that ringing again and look up to see Niki. Memories of the Staircase are returning.

She sadly smiles. Can she hear it too?

Goodbye Niki.

Staircase

Somehow I feel different after leaving the last door. The static that fills my head has a clarity I have never sensed before.

Staring at my hands, I notice they are dimly illuminated. But how? There is no sun. In fact, there is no light source at all. Yet my hands, no, everything somehow glows.

With a slight clearing of my mind I look up from the staircase, I see a thin ribbon traversing an empty, starless sky.

Funny, after all this time I have never looked up before. I can't help but wonder if I am seeing the staircase overhead.

In our endless march, I see it again. The sign "Girls, Girls, G_rls." Never have I seen the same door twice and yet here it was three times in a row.

The continuous flow prevents me from stopping. In a river of flowing people I stare at the door that quickly killed me twice. Hands pushing me to move forward and low grumbles from disgruntled zombies are too much for me to hang back.

This time, begrudgingly, I pass the door and go with the flow. A voice inside me wants to go back to see Niki. But here, in the Staircase, it is impossible to go against the flow.

After many miles of walking up the staircase I get over it. Finished with punishing myself, I become determined to grab the very next door regardless of what is on the sign.

The sign says, "Fighter Pilot." Always wanted to learn how to fly. I turn the rusty door handle and enter.

Portal 3

"I fear I may have underestimated reality as a dynamic unity. In my efforts to explain how energy can transfer through waves in space, I overlooked the possibility of energy transference between other dimensions. After giving away so many of my patents; this one I can not share."

- Excerpt from the lost papers of N.T. -

Fighter Pilot

The sun is setting on the tarmac. Blessed by the Shaman, my plane is ready for flight.

Sounds a little dramatic, I know, but this airplane and I are like one. An extension of my body.

Always excited to hop in my plane, I can't wait to see what I will accomplish this time. I feel so free when I fly.

Once in the air, I pull behind the leader of the squadron. The joystick is a little loose but no matter, I can manage. It is the nature of flight.

Getting familiar with the controls, my fingers dance over the controller. Settling into my seat, I can finally relax and enjoy the ride.

Rocking the plane back and forth, up and down is the true feeling of freedom. To be a bird with nothing but the wind hitting your face would be glorious.

Like living a dream, I pull the plane as close to the ocean swells as I can. Pulling back on the throttle, the waves feel incredibly fast beneath me.

Heading straight into a sunset, the sky is set ablaze with fiery red and orange. I skim the waves. My adrenaline rushes.

Flying through the night, the sun starts to rise. Brilliant pinks and yellows highlight the silvery clouds. The indescribable beauty fills my heart with peace.

A buzzer on my instrument panel catches my attention. We have been flying over the ocean for many hours without refueling.

"Fuel Near Empty," my attention becomes focused.

The leader of our squad tilts his wings, signaling us to follow. He banks down and hard right. There must be land nearby. As we get closer to the water our fearless leader tilts his wings again as if to salute and pulls out of formation. With our captain out of the way I can now see our target. The USS Nimitz.

No. This can't be.

I hit the instrument panel with my fists until they bleed.

Kamikaze pilots get scared too. The ship fills my view.

The sound of static fills my brain. No….Not again………

Staircase

The feeling of overwhelming despair fills my heart.

Each breath comes hard.

Is this everything? Is this what life is all about, risk?

I will try one more door but I will not be drawn in by some unknown force.

Out of defiance I enter the very next door.

The sign reads, "Cowboy".

Giddy up. Let's go.

Portal 4

"At night, my peripheral vision seems most acute. Stare at a star and it disappears. Look to the side and it jumps into my vision as a brilliant luminary. Stare at a person, he appears normal, shift my view to the side and he takes on a hue. Each person seems to have their own color. So far I seem to be the only one to see this."

- Excerpt from the lost papers of N.T. -

Cowboy

A chill fills the night air. As I wake, I can tell it is early. My back hurts from lying on the hard ground all night, I'm not used to this. I slowly open my eyes. The campfire had burnt out, but there is a partial moon and I can see my horse pulling at tuffs of grass.

I'm restless and can't sleep, so at first light I pack up and head out.

The trail will be long and torturous, but I've heard that at the end of it is a little "one horse town" of about 50 people…great place for a fresh start. No one will know me there. Perfect!

By late morning, I'm on the edge of town. The saloon is not hard to spot. There are only 5 buildings along the dusty main street. Actually, it's the only street, with the bar at dead center. And, as they say, "it's noon somewhere."

Pushing aside the swinging doors, I follow a well worn path in the old wood floor that leads to the bar. With a smile, I hear my spurs clink as I make my way to the empty stool directly in front of me. Looking in the mirror behind the bar, I see a scrawny, unshaven man in need of a real bath. Rubbing my hand over the stubble on my chin, I thought…Is that bum really me?

Thirst getting the better of me, my voice hoarse with dust, I rasp, "Bartender…a marti.-.a shot of whisky."

He's a big man, slow in his movements. His smile feels so familiar – so personal. Don't know why, I just rode into town, but it feels as though I should know this man.

Maybe his name is José…Bartenders are always called Joe or Bill, or Mac. Always a simple name.

He looks up, startled, as the o'le swinging door behind me creaks open a second time…….

"Who rode in on that Chestnut mare out front….?"

Now there's a voice I wouldn't buy a drink for.

Looking over my shoulder, I see he is staring straight at me, a squint and a glare in his eye, his bearing stiff and hostile. I say, "eye" as he is wearing a black patch over one, which only adds to his menacing appearance.

My horse is visible over his shoulder as the doors slowly swing shut. Without even giving me a chance to defend myself, he goes for his gun!

SHIT….The sign above the Stairway did not say "Horse Thief."

Lying on the cold floor, I hear the "all too familiar" sound of static. I already know what comes after that. I can't take this anymore. I'm done with the "adventure doors….PERIOD!"

The light begins to fade…the static……

Staircase

Defeated, without the will to continue, I give in once again
to the Staircase. Let the static lead me forever, I don't care.

I stay in a catatonic state. How long I don't know. Could
be a week or a hundred years. Doesn't matter. No way for
me to tell.

I just walk with unblinking eyes, a slow methodical pace.
Marching to the static that fills the mind. Senses numb.

Lost in my own thought, I fall into a particularly deep state
of despair. Just trying to close my eyes is difficult.
Please.....Some relief, even for a moment.

I hear the breathing next to me.

Quietly moving....going with the flow. In the playground
of my mind, I feel safe. Listen to the breathing.

Portal 5
Chimera

"In my dreams, everything is real. When awake, dreams are not real. On the basic quantum level, an enigma springs from the nothingness of empty thought. I cannot exist for I cannot be real, yet here I am."

- Excerpt from the lost papers of N.T. -

Sleep

In my bed. The pillow so soft. I had forgotten how
wonderful a down pillow covered with silk can feel.

My wife's' feet lay next to mine. There is warmth in that,
emotional as well as physical. My world is complete. My
mind is at ease. I feel safe.

Her breathing turns into a soft, small chirping noise. I
smiled to myself, amused at first.

Soon her soft chirping grows to a loud whistle; after many
minutes of listening it starts to irritate me. This is my first
real sleep, in I don't know how long, and I want to enjoy
it.

With every breath she takes. The whistling escalates.
Deep, soft inhale…noisy, rattling exhale. Over and over,
Hours seem to pass….in with the good air, out with the
noise…in with the good air, out with the noise…in with
the good air, out with the noise. Perfect pace. Ignoring is
impossible. That's it! I HAVE HAD IT. Good God, it has
got to stop!

At my wits end, I decide to nudge her into another position. I need to push just enough to disrupt her sound sleep and roll her onto her back.

Oops, I hit her a little too hard. Still sleeping, she moans in pain. I turn toward her to apologize.

Suddenly my breathing pattern changes and I hear my own nose chiming a different, softer note.

I laugh, "Dumb ass….I am my own irritant." A little embarrassed at myself I slowly fall back to sleep.

Static…..the numbing static.

Staircase

I open my eyes. Dream walking is a new experience.
Maybe that is why no one walks through the doors. Maybe
they are content with getting lost in their own thoughts.

Going with the flow once again. Shuffling past doors with
names like, San Francisco or Hiroshima. At least I am free
to choose how I want to die. New York....9/11...I don't
think so. The way my luck goes, I'd be the one jumping
from a burning building. Not my idea of a solo sport.

Riveocea, what an odd name. For some reason I feel drawn
to it but I am just not ready for another trauma. I have no
doubt that is what it would be. I pass it by.

Closing my eyes, I drudge on. The static numbs my mind.
Doing nothing seems more bearable.

A sense of peace comes over me. Lost in my own thoughts
I drift off......

The Bear

Standing on the edge of a precipice. My wife, Nichol, is leaning a little farther than I feel comfortable.

We peer over the edge of a 10-foot drop to get a better view of the long steep slope below. The bottom of the valley must be a thousand feet or more. And it's beautiful.

Nichol leans just a little too far and the gravel gives way under her feet. A look of horror plays across my face. My hand reaches out to grab her but all I feel is air…I am too late. After a hard landing, she begins a slow-motion slide, feet first. Rocks and grass slipping through her hands in a vain attempt to stop her fall. In a panic, she looks up to me for help….I have never felt so helpless in my life!

I soon realize that the only way I can be of any real help is to follow her down to the bottom and be there to help her with her injuries. Hopefully I can control my slide better than she did. Leaping and sliding, I follow her down.

Coming to an abrupt stop, my head is spinning. I take quick inventory, scratches and sore spots, but no broken bones.

From the trees I see a bear heading for Nichol at a full gallop.

Without thinking, I raise my arms into the air. Yelling and swinging my body about…anything to divert his attention from my wife; still numb and helpless from her tumble.

Looking toward me, the bear stops, rises up on his hind legs and gave a low angry growl that I could almost feel. My next move could well be my last.

I close my eyes and take a deep breath. I feel a vibration building inside my chest. A trembling feeling of power comes over me…a feeling I have never had before!

I open my eyes to face the bear. Instead, I see the ground getting farther and farther away from me. Slowly morphing into a giant, I tower twice the size of the bear.

I release another growl, louder and more fierce than the one before. The bear panics, turns, and runs back where he came from.

Suddenly my Nichol jumps on top of me shaking my shoulders frantically….She screams in my face, "Are you alright…are you alright…!"

Puzzled by my pleased expression she calms her panic, "That must have been one scary dream."

Drearily I respond, "Yeah…kind of. Did your hear me roar?"

"Oh god yes!"

Drifting back to sleep….. "Cool!"

Staircase

For the first time, in what seems like a long time, I am aware and feeling refreshed. I suddenly understand the staircase.

Dreams are just an escape from the Staircase. No need to enter doors and take a chance when you can get lost in your own dreams.

Many, caught in their own perpetual dreams, may never leave this place. It is easier to just follow, and become absorbed in your fantasies than to heal your soul and take on reality.

As vivid as the dreams are, they are just an easy escape.

It is easy to close my eyes to escape, but then it is all too tempting to get lost forever in Chimera.

I must try to avoid all dreams. I must focus on reality. I must figure out how to get out of here.

Now, I just spend my days in this endless routine. Walking, walking, walking.

Step by step. Moment to moment. I stare at my shuffling

feet. Never look up. Never look around and never, ever feel.

"Shoes that never wear out" I mumble, "a staircase that never ends......SHIT."

Many years have passed, or was it just yesterday since I have seen a door?

I am so tired of dying. So tired of ending up in this dungeon. If I could kill myself in the staircase I would do it. God knows I've tried.

There has to be something else.

My heart quickens when I glimpse a new door ahead.

Getting close I read a familiar sign. But this time the sign changed. In big bold letters the shape of musical notes, it reads 'RIVEOCEA'.

Again I try to resist the pull but it is stronger than I have ever felt. Almost irresistible.

A tone plays in my head...the first time I hear something other than the noise of the Staircase.

It's the same pure note that played when I left Niki at the bar. I hope some day to see her again.

I have chosen to bypass this door more times than I can remember. Moving toward the door I feel deep inside that this time, it could be different.

As I slowly open the door, I find I am actually looking forward to this adventure. With confidence I step through.

Portal 6
Riveocea

"The universe is Byzantine, yet we arrogantly state that we know how it will end, when in fact, it continues to grow more complex as we speak. Life has been a catalyst toward complexity. A living universe will always change the course of the inevitable. Does an ant know he lives in a forest? Dare we even guess what future awaits us?"

- Excerpt from the lost papers of N.T. -

Prologue

From the start this investigation stunk. This is just not my style. Why would they send me?

I work for a top-secret branch of the government. So secret that even the president of the United States does not know of our existence. But then again he doesn't know about many of our secret programs.

We monitor and infiltrate the intelligence community for oversight purposes. We have above top security clearance to ensure the constitutional freedoms are not lost.

Personally I have a hard time telling just who the bad guy really is. Who knows, it may even be me. At one time or another it could be all of us.

I am the best in my field yet can't remove this knot in my stomach. So many times I have wanted to just disappear into the humdrum life of a normal person. What I wouldn't give to get lost in my own little world and let someone else worry about all this security stuff.

That was about the time I got handed this job. It is a cold case and they want me to resolve it.

I would be insulted if they chose me to do what the portfolio says; "Find a runaway 16 year old." A simple Skip Tracy can find a 26 year old girl that ran away from home 10 years ago.

We even know what town she is in and calls herself Tess. How hard can that be? She must be the daughter of someone important to have me pulled in.

Riveocea, an odd name for a town nowhere near the ocean or even a river.

My legs are cramping and I'm tired from the long drive. I have a bad feeling about this case. Chalk that up to more years on the job than I care to admit.

Satellite images in the pre-op briefing show the small town of Riveocea to be a quaint farming village with very little outside commerce.

With the exception of calls from outside of town their phone chatter is almost nonexistent. This makes it impossible to get an accurate read on them.

Neighboring towns don't know much about Riveocea other than the common precept that the "town folk snub any and all outsiders." Some have accused it of being a cult but I guess I'll find out soon enough.

From the freeway the small exit sign to Riveocea looks more like a rustic wooden post with a cross nailed to it, or maybe it's just a sign for the loss of a loved one who died in a car crash.

Nope, it says "Riveocea 10 miles". By the looks of the gravel road they don't get a lot of company. The speed limit is 55 mph but 25 is all you can go without shaking the car to pieces and leaving a dust cloud for miles behind you.

The landscape is barren and foreboding. Great place to hide from the world.

A small stream washed out part of the road. Gaining a little speed allows me to skim across it without getting stuck.

The evening sun sets as I peak over the hill. What a pleasant surprise. The valley leading into the town is lush with flowering vegetation. Much more inviting than the barren wasteland I just drove through.

It is much larger than expected. There must be a 100,000 people living here.

According to the satellite images, it should have been a small burg of 5,000. I'll have to look into that oversight when I get back to the office.

I drive slowly through town looking for anything that seems out of place.

A narrow two lane highway lined with trees—a single hotel, a small shopping center, gas station, school....all very ordinary. A small-town feel, despite its large population. No blaring horns or dodging taxis. The people walking were calm and unhurried.

Looking for a sign to get my bearings, I realize that at every intersection there are no signs of any kind. No speed signs. No stop signs. No parking signs. Nothing.

The auto, bicycle and foot traffic all seem to flow

smoothly without traffic signs. Weird.

Near the center of town I finally spot the community center. A small, unassuming brick building with an old Schwinn bicycle leaning up against it.

That is usually the best place to ask questions without creating suspicion. A light was on so hopefully someone will be inside.

The stone walkway leads to an open lobby where an elderly gentleman stands. Holding the picture to his face I ask, "Have you seen this girl?"

He stares at me; actually, not at me but through me. After a long uncomfortable pause he puts on a plastic smile and says, "She is not here, but she will be with you in a moment. Would you like to see the community park while you wait?"

Surprised by his response, I stumble with my words, "Uh, well yes, thank you."

A little strange to say the least...oh well.

It will be a new record for me if I find her at the first place I stop and the first person I ask.

In back of the Center the 'Community Park' consists of a few roses in the middle of a gravel circle. The smell from the roses is intoxicating.

From the building, the elderly gentleman escorted me to the center of the town. He was pleasant enough but he obviously was trying to delay me.

In the center of town is a large, round water fountain lit by colored lights. Water trickles from a perfectly formed sculpture of someone they thought was important. Around the fountain are pedestrians and bicyclists, gathered like an important event was about to take place.

Behind the fountain is a giant brass, flag pole. 4 feet in diameter at the base extending 75 feet tall and tapering to 6 inches with a large brass ball at the very top.

Very impressive.

For a brief moment the man stops talking. It is a long enough pause for me to look up and notice the TV billboards. They are everywhere.

Sound and video comes from the billboards. Every TV is tuned to the same station. It is some sort of infomercial but I can't tell what they're selling.

Suddenly, as if choreographed, in one motion, the people stop and turn to face me. All of them.

Making an empty circle around me, they hold what looked like a combination of a 22 cal. pistol and a kids' air gun.

Realizing the serious situation I try to calm myself. "Don't panic."

All the billboard infomercials turn off in unison. Cars, bikes and pedestrians were all stopped and staring at me holding GUNS.

Holding the palms of my hands out facing the ground to suggest peace I exclaim, "Jesus, don't panic," hoping to calm the situation.

A small commotion rose behind the mob. The crowd split in an orderly rehearsed fashion to form an isle where one person could pass through.

And there she is. The girl in the picture. Tess moves from the back of the crowd to the front of the line.

Facing me, she calmly said, "You have created a disturbance in the community."

I may have underestimated this community. I have seen this situation before and usually you don't walk away from it. I braced for the worst.

My survival instincts kicked in, but there are too many of them. They all started firing their pistols. I was hit from all sides.

I went to the ground on my knees. In shock I look down to see that I am totally covered in small silver pellets. They stuck to my clothing and my skin, with no blood.

Out of relief, I uncontrollably begin to laugh. My laughing turns to tears and a feeling of confusion. This is the oddest thing I have ever experienced.

The crowd smiles in unison and starts to disperse. Tess didn't move. She stayed till they were all gone. "I hear you were looking for me....we need to talk," she said.

As she approaches a warming sensation starts at my feet, creeps up my leg. By the time it reaches my chest, I am overwhelmed with emotion.

Soon it encompassed my entire body; I am euphoric. I am

not drunk but it is the best feeling unimaginable. Could I have been drugged?

Tess comes closer, aimed the gun at my head and says, "You really are special you know."

She fires the gun and I fall to the ground. I hear the blood pump in my neck. A familiar static sound, then a note of crystal purity.

"No. Not now" I moan.

My last thought before losing consciousness is, "I don't want to go."

I slowly wake up expecting to hear shuffling of feet. Surprised to find I am still in Riveocea, I felt relief until I realize I could not move.

I'm not sure what the Staircase is, but I somehow know that I should not be able to remember it. Even now I can feel the memory begin to fade.

Without moving or opening my eyes I can feel the bindings around my feet and hands. Someone is breathing quietly near my bed.

My clothes feel soft, like pajama wear. Obviously they stripped me of my clothing and put me in some sort of hospital gown. All things considered I feel strangely alert and healthier than I have for a long time.

The breathing next to me falters slightly. A woman speaks, "I know you are awake."

I had hoped to learn more before I opened my eyes. It didn't work. Tess was sitting on the end of the bed.

"I also know you work for the government and was sent in

to find me. You know everything about me and my prior life as an outsider, but you know nothing of my life here in Riveocea. So, let's start fresh, shall we?"

Her face changed to a smile, "Hi, my name is Tess, what is your name?"

"My name is Bond, James Bond" I respond.

She laughs, "That's really funny. I'll bet a name like that is hard to live up to in your line of work."

"Yea" I grudgingly snap, "Just call me Jimmy."

"OK James, I know you have many questions. The community has agreed that I will be your escort and answer any questions while you are visiting us. What is your first thought?"

I ask, "What the hell did you people shoot me with? Did you drug me?"

I try to sit up but can't because of the restraints. "When can I get these things off."

"In time," she said, "We are not in a hurry."

In answer to your first question, "We shot you with a bot-dispenser."

Second question, "No we didn't drug you. The pellets you saw contain nano-bots. Small machines that enter your blood stream to scan and cure your body from diseases and such. We don't want you contaminating us.

The bot report told us you needed a liver repair because

you drink too much. Your knees were injured from a shooting accident. Do you want me to continue?"

"No, I get the picture."

I started to speak but she continued, "Unfortunately, I was also the one authorized by the community to administer the bot that knocked you out.....sorry about that"

Looking at my restraints, I question, "What now?"

"I know you came here to find me. I will answer all your questions within 24 hours and then you must leave," Her voice had a serious tone that gave me a chill.

"I would be more than pleased to show you my city." She answered, "We have much to offer someone like you. You are very special."

The offer was odd, almost as though she knows me; *no, like she really knew m*e. I replied, "I don't have much of a choice, do I?"

She giggles with a grin on her face, "No...you don't."

Untying my hands and feet she continues, "The rules are simple. You are free to go anywhere in the city, but you must be with me at all times. You can ask any questions and I will answer them as best I can. You must never disturb the harmonics of the community. I will let you know if that is happening."

Unfamiliar with her term, I interrupt, "you mean the harmony?"

She paused and mumbled under her breath, "Noob," then

49

continued, "No doubt you will understand more fully by the end of your stay.

"Your clothes are clean and folded in the closet. The GPS tracking devices have been taken out of your pants and coat. We will keep your spy pen, watch and glasses until you are ready to leave. I will be waiting outside the door when you are dressed and ready to go.

"Any questions?"

"Oh yeah. One question. When do I get one of those guns?"

Laughing softly she stands up, shakes her head, then, without a word, leaves.

It is almost midnight with a full moon when I open the door. Tess is waiting for me outside the building.

To my surprise she said, "As a token of good faith I am presenting you with your own personal Bot-dispenser. Use it wisely.

"No one else can use your new BD. It is programmed to your personal frequency.

"It is fully functional with only the recycle-bot disabled. It is a one of a kind. Keep it with you at all times. Do not, I repeat, do not lose it."

On closer examination it looks more like an empty silver tube rather than a gun. "How does it work?"

I couldn't help but wonder how they came up with this kind of technology. Nothing like this exists outside of this town. Believe me, I know. That's my job in the Government. Could they have found some alien technology?

"All you have to do is think a happy thought and a happy-bot will shoot."

Wow, a gun that is triggered by thought; the mystery of this place goes deep. I have really underestimated these people.

Remembering yesterday's experience with the pleasure bots, I pointed the BD at my arm hoping to reproduce that same euphoric feeling; minus the fainting, of course.

Tess laughed, "Don't be silly, you cannot pleasure yourself. First timers always try but the bots are made for the benefit of the community, not self.

"You asked earlier about Harmonics. It is much like the light spectrum. However, Harmonics is on a much grandeur scale. An electromagnetic spectrum that has an infinite number of frequencies and the light we see with our eyes is only a small portion of its frequencies. It is the energy from life itself. Each living person has their own frequency within the Harmonics.

"We all are different colors of the same spectrum so to speak. Because we each have our own frequency, the bots can tune into our special tone."

"Can you read my thoughts?"

"No, not really. It's more like seeing your intent or feeling your motives. For us in Riveocea it is another form of communication. And even though you do not have the skills yet, your connection with the harmonics is very strong."

"How can you know that? I can't even hear it." Her mouth curved in a smile, "For all good things you must wait."

She continued, "The frequency cannot be heard as you

52

think of hearing. Our brains here in Riveocea sense it. Everyone in the Community sends the signal as well as receives it. Together we create a blend that balances the Harmonics.

"A piano can play one note or several. No one wants to hear a note out of tune. You are out of tune. We sense it and it causes a small imbalance in our Harmonics, but that can be corrected. You cannot hear us because you do not believe. Once you accept us, the symphony will begin."

I shot back, "You mean I will be able to read your mind?"

"Noob!"

"Why do you call me that?"

"I just mean you're special." Tess whispers in my ear.

"Where did your community learn about Harmonics?"

"All in good time." She murmured.

Still confused, I drop the conversation. Let's move on to researching this odd town.

Some of what she said did make sense. Sometime in my past, I do remember hearing a ringing; a note so pure I thought I must have heard it in a dream. Now I am not so sure. The memory of the note seems much clearer now.

I wish I could remember.

I must admit, there is something very intriguing about these people.

We walked all night. We talked. Tess showed me different parts of Riveocea and never held back answering my questions.

Most of the town is unremarkable. But, the nature of what they call the Harmonics still eludes me. It seems to bring comfort to their town.

I have never felt this safe before. There is a level of trust here that I have yet to understand.

As we walk through the streets, I can tell the people are at peace. No pushing or shoving. Everyone has places to go but no one is in a hurry.

We pass a street vendor selling fruits and vegetables. Tess reaches out, grabs an apple and keeps walking. I stop and scold her, "you forgot to pay for that."

"Did I forget to mention we don't have money here? Everything is free."

Bewildered I respond, "Everything?"

"Yes, everything. The cars, our homes, the food, the clothing, everything!"

Then I see a young kid driving a sports car down the street. Snidely I say, "What about that kid in the Tesla sports car, surely that's not free."

Tess laughs, "That's Bobby. He is a Noob but he will learn."

Oh, is he special too?" I interrupts.

With a quirky smile she continues, "Most of the new kids want to live in a mansion up the hill and drive fancy cars. The mansions were built for anyone to use."

"They can live there as long as they want. Once they are fully integrated into the Harmonics they come to realize that those things don't matter here. I give him six months of living the high life before he calms down. That's what makes a free society really special."

Spotting a liquor store, I walk through the doors, Grabbing a fifth of gin off the shelf, I slowly inch my way out the door.

As I reach for the door knob I look back at the clerk to see his reaction. Fully expecting the clerk to ask me to pay for it, he waves to me instead and said, "Have a nice day!"

Wow!!! This is way too much information for me to take in at one time.

Opening the bottle, I take a big gulp of gin. I grumble under my breath, "There is no such thing as a free society."

"Are you hungry for breakfast?" Tess asked.

"Starving"

We walked in silence. I tried to collect my thoughts. Tess is starting to grow on me. I even love the gentle sway of her infectious walk. I catch her humming a vaguely familiar song. How odd.

It took 10 minutes to reach the restaurant. A quaint European style building. The architecture was simple on the outside but very elegant inside.

Outside of Riveocea this would have been a very expensive restaurant. Hard to believe breakfast is going to free.

Sitting down I peruse the menu, which has very authentic Italian cuisine.

For breakfast they, of course, serve Italian Breakfast Milk (Cappuccino), orange juice and a Cornetto. Italians eat a light breakfast but they never want you to leave hungry.

Our waitress evokes memories of Sophia Loren with her Italian sway and wit. Her beauty seems to glow accenting her olive skin through her black formal gown. Of course her low cut neckline doesn't hurt.

Standing as if showing off her body, she shrugs one shoulder. As if reading my mind utters her first words, "I owe it all to spaghetti," one of Sophia's famous quotes.

She bent down to place the napkin in my lap. Leaning over way too far, I see her breasts exposed more than I feel comfortable. She asks, "Would you like our Italian breakfast?"

I must have stared at her beautiful cleavage a little too long. Embarrassed, I stutter a little and say, "Yes, that will be fine." Looking down at my lap, I see the BD in my hand.

Before the thought even gels in my mind, a pellet shoots to her neckline.

The waitress stands up a little surprised. Pauses for a moment, closes her eyes, takes a deep breath and exhales slowly.

I am a little apprehensive. Her face flush, she looks down at me and leans over to reveal her breasts again. Her face close to mine I see her soft, loving eyes and a beautiful smile. She kisses her slender fingers, brushes them against my cheek and says, "Thank you."

A little embarrassed I looked at Tess. She gives me a knowing smile and a wink.

"Congratulations, that was your first pleasure-bot."

The two hours in the restaurant went by quickly. I am beginning to understand why people never leave this place.

Walking past a garden area, I wonder; can anything really be this perfect?

The people walk, work and live in perfect harmony together. As if in a vacation resort, a stroll through the streets of Riveocea makes me feel as though I have not a care in the world.

Spotting another billboard, it occurred to me; if everyone communicates with each other, why do they need the billboard infomercials?

Without my even having to ask the question Tess explains, "We use them as information bulletins when work needs to be done in the community. A volunteer sends a note to the Matriarchs who then coordinate the project."

"You don't just think it?"

"No," said Tess, "We try not to clutter the Harmonics with unnecessary thoughts."

"Matriarchs....What Matriarchs?" I asked.

"We do need things to be organized. Our Community chose three of our most respected and balanced people to oversee our higher functions. They help maintain our individual harmonics.

"With their help," she continued, "we do not experience too much chatter in our heads. Too many people talking at the same time can get confusing. Too many people asking for help causes a singularity in the frequency. Does that make sense?"

A 'singularity in the frequency', sounds like she is speaking a different language. I could only squeak out. "Uhh, yea I guess."

"Let me explain it this way. People outside Riveocea all 'want' things for themselves. Unless a catastrophe occurs they rarely think of the needs of others. They work hard and they want to be paid for it. Money allows them to purchase things and own things. When you get a thousand individuals all wanting their own things, the Harmonics gets completely out of tune.

"That is what we call a singularity in the frequency."

"Okay, Okay," I snap, "in other words, we outsiders are selfish."

"True but not quite the point. If you take those same thousand people and give them all one purpose like we have in the Community, take care of their immediate necessities, then the workload for each individual diminishes. As a community they spend more time fulfilling their lives with meaningful endeavors whether that be inventing and creating works of art, or just helping others. Don't you see, life in the Harmonics fulfills our personal desires but together we can easily………"

"Stop!" I interrupt, "My head is spinning. I don't want to talk about this anymore."

I need to clear my thoughts if I am going to understand this place.

Very few things are really coincidental. Which makes me wonder why, at that precise moment, the TV billboard starts announcing a corn harvest at the Pederson Ranch.

Maybe working beside them in one of their larger projects will help. I ask Tess, "Care to do some farming?"

It took a half hour to reach the edge of the Pederson ranch. I can see hundreds of people swarming the field.

There appears to be no foreman nor did it look like they needed one. It was like watching bees in a hive.

Swiftly and efficiently they clear the field. Everyone is working at a deliberate fast pace, with no mistakes. No bumping into each other or dropping baskets of husked corn.

Feeling out of place, I am the only one who is clumsy and working at a much slower pace than everyone else. I am the only person that does not quite fit in.

Before I knew it the field was clean. With a little hard work and fresh air in my lungs, I feel good.

Everyone took some corn home for dinner, and a large basket was going to be delivered to the market. The rest is going into storage.

Tess asks me if I want to take some home. I respond, "No."

"OK, but you might want to stay and watch the recycle-bot do his job."

Tess must have assumed that I knew what a recycle-bot did since she disabled it from my bot-gun. I have no clue what to expect.

This could get interesting. I might want one for myself.

She walks over to the corn husk pile and holds her BD in the air. One small pellet shoots onto the pile and it instantly starts to disintegrate.

A wave of dust travels across the field and when it was done there was no sign of the corn, husks or even the stalks. It was all gone….Nothing left but dirt.

I take some in my hand and bring it to my nose. It has the feel and smell of a high quality potting soil.

Tess kneels on one knee, holds her head down and prays, "Ashes to ashes, dust to dust."

Did everyone in the Community have such respect for the earth?

How many problems could be eliminated if the outsiders got a hold of this technology, but also what damage would be caused from its misuse?

Realizing my thoughts, it disturbed me that I was starting to refer to my own people as "outsiders".

The sun is getting low in the sky. Relaxed, I stare at the many colors the sun was throwing onto the clouds. Why haven't I done this more often? It is beautiful and so relaxing.

We walk in silence for quite some time before Tess asks, "Don't you get lonely in your head when you can't feel the others around you?"

"No."

She continues, "If you could sense the Harmonics. It's like a warm blanket surrounding your body on a cold night. Once you feel the comfort you cannot live without it."

I sternly bark, "No thank you, I like my privacy. How do you cope with your loss of privacy?"

Even as the words came out of my mouth, I feel the hypocrisy. On the outside, it was my job to spy on people and get their communities to spy on each other so I could gather intelligence.

Can't tell you how many times my community policing

efforts turned into small town bickering and excuses for settling a grievance against a neighbor. The difference here is trust. Trust that information will not be abused.

In the back of my mind, I can't help but wonder if it is possible to have enough trust in each other that loss of privacy would be meaningless. I am beginning to hope she is right.

While still in deep thought she abruptly announces, "Your 24 hours are up."

She sounds disappointed. "I will take you to your apartment, gather your personal items, and you are free to leave."

I explored all 24 hours without bothering to sleep and yet I needed more time. "What?" I raise my voice hoping for a delay, "You mean… I'm not even tired. It could not have gone that fast."

Under her breath she whispers, "Afraid so." She looks up at me with puppy dog eyes and a tear running down her face.

I think she is truly going to miss me.

At the condo she gives back my keys to the car, all my personal effects, and a bonus kiss on the cheek. Then walks to the door.

"Wait," I exclaim, "one last question. What if I join your community?"

Looking at me with a glimmer of hope she says, "Hold the gun to your head and shoot a transition-bot." She gives me a small smile.

Starting to close the door she adds, "But please, don't do it unless you are sure. You are special so I know you will make the right decision."

With that she left. The door seemed to shut behind her without effort.

I sit on the edge of the bed for what seems hours, just staring at the gun.

Like a roller coaster, my emotions vacillate between my wanting to run away and get my private life back or give in to the draw of what they call the Harmonics.

Clearing my mind as I often do when a particularly difficult decision needs to be made, I sit in meditation.

Calling on something deep inside me, my final hunch is usually correct. Relying on my gut, the decision is made.

Suddenly, I hold the gun to my head, close my eyes, and concentrate.

Riveocea
Chapter 10

My head starts to spin. My eyes blur and the top of my head itches. I hear a white noise; the very familiar sound of static.

Like watching a TV turned to an off channel, except I see the noise. Fear wells up inside of me. I only hear this sound of static. I am not ready to leave Riveocea.

Mosquito noises start to whirl around my head. Becoming louder each time it circles my head, the volume becomes intense, almost unbearable.

Feeling like my head is going to explode; the static lowers` an octave. Uncomfortable yes, but bearable.

Images enter my head, then flashes of pattern that turn to shadows. Almost like a hallucinogenic drug, strobe lights flash.

Trying to remain calm, I reflect on my last encounter with a bot pellet and know the effects will be temporary.

Once again my head feels as though it's about to explode. No sense of time and no sense.....at all. No touch, smell, feel or sound....just the.......vibration of the whispers.

The mosquito sounds; the pictures in my head all start to make sense. The volume rises till I thought I was going to pass out.

Closing my eyes seems to keep the spinning at a minimum. In my head I can see the patterns turn to a ribbon of light across the sky. Like a never-ending rainbow. Life seems clear if only for a moment. It is dim and colorless at first. I try to focus. The colors become vivid and the sound lowers another octave.

I now can see small vibrations of the unfamiliar colored bands of a strange rainbow dancing to a tuning fork.

The mosquito buzzing sound morphs into cackling geese. As the cackling geese fade, small voices call to me from the air.

They seem to coordinate with the vibrating cords of the rainbow. I feel as if I am growing a new set of eyes and ears inside my head.

Finally, seeing it in full view, the static is gone. I know this is the Harmonics. Not only beautiful; it shimmers off everything I see. I always wondered what a new color would look like. Now I know.

All the oscillating colors and voices coordinate into what feels like a giant orchestra making one great harmonic practice cord at the beginning of a concert. Without some kind of order to the Harmonics, I see it could drive you mad.

With my eyes open I can hear and see the community,

where they are in relation to me, see their mood and hear their thoughts. The overall feeling is true love and it feels good.

The power of this new vision scares me. It is the perfect surveillance weapon. How the outside world could abuse it. They might even destroy themselves.

No wonder Riveocea has isolated itself.

I sense on the first band of color someone moving toward me. I feel the emotion and eventually hear the excited voice.

It is Tess.

She bursts through the door, runs toward me and jumps onto me. I fall back on the bed with her on top of me. She kisses all over my face.

No words are necessary. She feels what I feel. Now I see what she sees. We are two notes playing in perfect harmony.

"I knew you would do it."

She pauses for a moment, and lovingly kisses me on the lips.

We both know where we are going with this.

In fact, so does the rest of the Community.

Riveocea
Chapter 11

Waking up the next morning, Tess is not in the room. I can feel her presence. Closing my eyes, all my senses scream "Breakfast for Two". She waits for me at a small restaurant around the corner.

Looking in the window of the restaurant, I see people sitting around our table. The side of Tess's mouth curves as she waves for me to come in.

Everyone is busy with their own conversations, ordering food and eating, but the Harmonics knows. They are all a buzz about Tess and I as a couple and what happened last night.

I ask Tess, "Does it bother you that everyone knows what happened last night?"

Still smiling she says, "You'll get used to it. What we did last night was an act of passion between us.

The Harmonics was shared, not the passion. The community felt the elation much like a pleasure bot and it united us and gave us a shared purpose. Feeling good and sharing our joy is our way........"

I blankly stare for a moment but I know she is right.

"Let me explain another way. When two Noobs fall in love… you do know what a Noob is now?"

"Of course I do; and it feels good not to be an outsider."

"Anyway, they know their soul mates are driven to share their profound love.

"The problem is the only avenue they know of is procreation. The baby cements their bond.

"The Harmonics expands the desire to bond, on a grand scale. Everyone shares the unity, love and peace. We all benefit."

A flash memory of the Staircase bursts into my mind. "Is this real?" I wonder. The recalled memories disturb me greatly and I can tell it creates a small disturbance in the Harmonics.

Tess reaches up and gently touches my hand. "I know," She says consolingly, "there is a reason for the Static. We still don't understand it but we share the sadness."

Two months of living in the Community and I am still not trained for anything special. It is a bit humbling to be average when I was the best of the best as a Noob.

Although Tess keeps telling me I am unique, you can't tell it by my job. I think I should be content for a while just being a "jack of all trades". There is plenty of time to decide how I fit in.

Up at the mansion, Bobby is getting tired of his roadster. I know a little mechanics and Bobby's car needs some fine tuning. That will be fun.

What a fine automobile. The 2010 Tesla Roadster. The first, truly fast, all electric sports car. With 288 horse power and a top speed of 125 miles per hour, it will go from 0-60mph in 3.7 seconds. All that speed with 0 emissions. I am having fun just cleaning it.

Bobby comes up from behind and asks me, "Do you like it?"

"It's a beaut,"

"It's yours," he replies. He is a fast learner. It only took him two months. I accepted his offer because, well, no one else needs it right now.

That evening, as I detail the interior, I open the battery box and see nothing. Where there should be 300 pounds of battery, there is one 12v battery, a small box containing some electronics and two antennae that looks like upside down swizzle sticks with a ball on top of each.

"What the hell is this?"

At that moment Tess calls to me to meet her at the community center. She must sense my confusion. Her message is hard to understand … something about a history lesson.

I finish wiping down the car and grab a bike to make my way into town. Didn't take the car to avoid being call a Noob.

On the way back to town I notice all the electric cars being driven. There are a lot of them. At second glance I notice everyone drives electric cars. The only gas powered cars are driven by the Noobs. This history lesson is going to be interesting.

Waiting for me behind the fountain past the giant flag pole, she proudly stands at the entrance of what looks like a two hundred year old building. Its steel spires point to the sky.

I shake my head with a quirky smile. All the walks we took in this town and she never took me here. I wonder why?

The architecture looks like late 19th century Serbian or Croatian. What on earth is that doing here?

Tess opens the giant steel gates with a heavy push. There's

a dull squeaking as the hinges turn, like it had not been opened for years.

As if she were a tour guide, she starts to explain, "My great, great, grandfather built this building."

Walking toward the antique doors, she continues, "His name was Robert Underwood Johnson. He worked as a diplomat for the US government and was good friends with Nikola Tesla."

As the doors swing open I see a plaque on the wall that reads, "This building dedicated to the Memory of N.T."

We enter the ancient building. The room is empty except for a black-coated steel spiral staircase leading down under the building.

"This is more my speed," I mutter as I take the lead to the room at the bottom of the stairs. "I can't wait to see what's down here."

"Wait for me," Tess calls.

Reaching the door, I fling it open to see…. an empty room.

With an obvious look of disappointment, I turn to say something when I feel a vibration on the floor. It seems to emanating from all around me. I touch the walls feeling the same vibration; Tess must have seen my shocked look when she flipped on the lights.

The room is made entirely of black steel and giant rivets. It looks like an ancient submarine.

Within the Harmonics, looks of surprise are rare. Savoring

the moment, she sighs and after a long pause says, "Beneath us is an underground river. It is the sole source of power for the city."

She crosses the floor with a skeleton key in a teasing fashion; she very slowly inserts the key into the only locked door in the room.

It wouldn't surprise me if this is the only locked door in Riveocea. I hear the lock click. She stops, looks back at me to build my anticipation then gently pushes the door open. Dim lights made it hard to see. The low vibration turned to loud machinery noises. How can they keep such large machinery hidden from us?

From the sounds, I know the machine has to be big but when I peek around the corner I am awestruck by the sheer size of it.

Taking one step into the room, the platform I am standing on is 50 feet higher than the floor. The room itself is the size of a football field with no structural pillars supporting the ceiling span.

My stomach churns a little as Tess presses a button on the handrail to lower the platform to the ground. I hear water flowing through the hydraulic pipes around me as the platform drops.

"I feel like I am in a Jules Verne novel."

Tess smiles, "You are."

"He was hired by Grandpa Johnson to design this structure."

Speechless, I just stand there staring at the wonder in front of me as the platform stops on the bottom floor. This must be a very ancient wonder. It is truly an amazing sight.

Overwhelmed, I remain speechless. Examining the brass labels I realize that it is technology from 130 year ago and it surpasses anything we have today. And I had clearance to see it all.

I was finally starting to understand just how complex this community really is.

Tess shouts over the top of machinery noises, "These two large cylinders are bladeless turbines. It uses a boundary layer affect coined by Tesla. In the simplest of terms it uses the friction from water flowing under the machinery to spin the shaft. It's the same principle used in an aircraft wing except, in this case, the water is much more viscous."

"This is all way over my head".

She does not hear me and continues, "The generator spins and creates a 'standing wave' of electricity that is projected by the brass pole in front of this building. In short it creates electricity that travels though the air. And needs no wires. All you need is a receptor in your vehicle or home to receive the electricity projected by the generator."

Thinking to myself; "I haven't seen any power lines in town either, this begins to make more sense."

"I have heard about some of Nikola Tesla's experiments but his standing wave technologies never materialized. Why would they have it here?"

Speaking loudly as we walk, "Tesla introduced his technology to the government and soon after, lost the contract bid to Edison. At that point he realized that corrupt politics, corporate greed, government power and the military were the driving forces behind all important decisions.

"Tesla wanted electricity, for that matter, all his inventions to be free to the people. He was so disappointed in the system that he withdrew all his notes and studies from prying, government eyes. He handed his papers to Grandpa Johnson and made him promise not to release them until the world was ready for it.

"Grandpa agreed, with the stipulation that he could, in secret, build one standing wave machine. Tesla agreed, and that is what you are looking at."

As we walk through the immense field of machinery and noise, Tess continues with her history lesson.

This is all so overwhelming. So much to absorb.

Eventually, we finish the tour at the other end of the facility and enter what seems to be the only door in the entire complex. We enter the room and Tess shuts the door behind me. All the noise is gone.

I have only one question, "Why did you show this to me now?"

"Because you are special, I told you that the first day I saw you."

All can say is, "Explain."

"We don't know for sure why, but your Harmonic note is more pure than anything we have seen since Tesla himself. What that means, or what you are capable of we are not really sure.

"We do know you need training. We need to see what happens when you are completely in tune with the Harmonics."

She pauses, "It can be good or bad but we know you are special."

I didn't feel special but I am not going to let an opportunity like this pass by.

The room is filled with books lining the walls. At the center of the room sits one table and three chairs.

I thought to myself. "This seems to be a study room for the Matriarchs."

"You are correct" Tess answers. I keep forgetting she can

feel what I am thinking. She continues, "This is where the leaders of the community consult Tesla's notes to continue his studies."

"Can I read the books?"

"That is why I brought you here. To develop to your potential, you will need to understand Nikola Tesla's theories.

"These books are for anyone to read," she replies, "This is a free society where there are no secrets and information is for every one of us to use. Unfortunate for most of us, only someone who's harmonics are extremely pure can make full use of this knowledge."

Wow. I start walking along the walls and reading the book titles and looking at pictures of prior Matriarchs placed intermittently among the books. Tess calls me back, "Please sit down at the table. There is more you must know before you start reading."

Her tone is serious as she explains, "Once Tesla's standing wave tower was built and running at full capacity, the Community started seeing anomalies in the electric waves. The wave generator emitted an unknown resonance.

"It was an unexplained frequency that led us to understanding Harmonics on a quantum level. With that discovery, and lots of experimentation, we were able to adjust our brainwaves to hear and see these harmonics."

I still do not quite understand, "you mean if I left this town I could no longer see the harmonics."

"Not exactly" she explains further, "all humans have the

capacity to see on the minor quantum level, they just don't know what it is."

Tess could see the puzzled look still on my face, "have you ever had a dream so vivid that you were startled awake?"

"Yes, often."

"That is, in its simplest form, a singularity in the quantum level. What we have accomplished is enhancing everyone's singularity and combining it into a sound wave our brains can see and hear." She carefully formed her words as she said, "If you leave, you will retain much of your new talent but you will revert to a singular level. We have found abuse of Harmonics power in the singular, used outside this town, too tempting for anyone to resist. For your protection, our protection and the worlds' protection, small trips outside this town are acceptable. But you must always come back."

"Has anyone ever really wanted to leave?"

"Only one," she sounds upset, "He had a very pure tone but he left Riveocea and his loneliness and power on the quantum level eventually drove him mad. You would know him as Adolph Hitler. He caused a great disturbance in the Harmonics."

Not to mention what he did to the outside world, I thought.

Staring at her silently, I could tell she is visibly shaken. It takes her some time to compose herself. She continues, "He is terribly missed in the harmonics and until he left, we never quite realized just how dangerous we could be to the outside world."

I ask, "How can you miss him? He died in 1942."

"Even though you die, your life force can be imprinted, on the quantum level, into the Harmonics. All his knowledge, actions, and feelings could have continued through the harmonics. His life is now in the static level with the rest of the outsiders."

"When he died, outside the Tesla barrier of Riveocea. All that he was is gone. He wasted his life." She sat quietly staring at the wall without expression, when a small tear rolled down her cheek.

I gathered my thoughts before responding, "I know the entire Community took a chance by letting you show me this. Thank you so much for the tour. This is one of the most enlightening days of my life. I understand the dangers of knowledge and power in the wrong hands, and I will do everything in my power to protect this secret from falling into the wrong hands." I hesitate, "but, much of our powers are already utilized by the government and with constitutional protections, the citizens are protected from any abuse."

Tess, disturbed by my comment, silently stands up and leaves the room. I follow her to the platform and we leave the building.

She kisses me on the cheek and says, "I love you, let's go home."

Almost a year has passed since I started my studies of the Tesla files. I can now clearly see the Harmonics of others.

I find it interesting that I can shift my Harmonics to match others, though it seems to have no real purpose. However, it makes for good conversation at the community center.

I received help from a couple of the physicists, one was a Matriarch, and spent the last two months trying to understand all the Tesla documents.

My knowledge has grown and I have discovered a few new promising ways to apply Harmonics. In practice they haven't worked out yet.

I hope to find a safe way to test them soon.

Rifling through a few of Tesla's last files, I run across two pages that are brittle but appear to be his last log.

Hard to decipher, the last page jumps out at me. He had drawn a large never ending mobius strip and labeled it "static harmony". He left the paper unfinished.

Just on the edge of memory, the words on the tip of my tongue. My lips move in astonishment as I realize what it is, "The Staircase."

Riveocea
Chapter 15

Late in the day while finishing a remodel on my neighbors' kitchen, I feel a disturbance in the harmonics. The community calls me to the community center.

Walking to Town, I sense some urgency. A bike rider pulls beside me and hands me his bike.

A Noob is asking for me and flashing my picture to the community. I knew this day would come just as Tess had been expecting me.

Another Agent is snooping around town, only this time they are tracking me.

I am not going fast enough. As soon as I had this thought, Bobby drives up behind me and stops. He grabs the bike and hands me the keys to the roadster. Without words he projects the need for urgency.

As I approach the crowd surrounding the Snoop, they have her surrounded with their bot-dispensers drawn.

Remembering my first day here, I realize how terrified she must be. The community feels my presence. The crowd split apart to allow me access to the center of the circle.

I sense her fear. She is a young recruit. In her mid twenties and of slender build. Probably expendable. I am sure head quarters was tired of losing experienced agents to this community.

I approach the newcomer and say, "I hear you've been looking for me."

With a trembling voice she whispers, "What did I do?"

There is no way for her to understand, but I try anyway, "By coming here looking for me, you have created a disturbance in the community."

The entire community shoots their BD at the same time. I shoot the bot that knocks her out.

Reaching down to pick her up, I know what I have to do, and I only have 24 hours to do it.

Her name is Sara. Fresh out of training, a little overzealous, but that is normal. She wants to prove to HQ that she is worthy of being a "special agent in charge".

She may be a little more difficult for us recruit.

I showed her the town following the same protocol as Tess did with me. The 24 hour tour finished without incident. I am disappointed how few questions she asked. Evidently her mind is fixed on the job.

I sent her to the same hotel room I was in to contemplate her future. After 45 minutes she leaves her room and walks to the community center where I wait for her. Handing me her BD she says, "This will make a very interesting report."

"Are you sure?" I plead, "this is a once in a lifetime opportunity for you. You can live in a totally free society……. Are you very sure?"

I have a bad feeling when she quickly responds, "Yes."

The Harmonics surges. We have never been rejected by a

Noob once we show them our way of life. The community is humming in my head with voices from everyone; "We must protect the community." "She cannot leave with the knowledge of us." "Why would anyone reject us?" "What do we do?"

One Matriarch finally spoke up, "For the benefit of the community, she must be recycled."

"Recycled?" I scream in my head. "But this is a free society. We have the freedom to do anything we want, including freedom to choose not to live this way."

It is repeated, "For the benefit of the community, for the benefit of the world, you must use the recycle-bot."

I scream again, only this time using my singular tone, "I refuse!"

Surrounded with bot-dispensers set on recycle. I feel their intent and they feel mine. Self preservation would cause them to recycle both of us. Self-preservation would cause me to react.

They can feel everything I am about to do except my new found knowledge. I have to use it now.

I had hoped to test Tesla's theory first. I could end up stranded forever.

I hear pops from BDs. No time for tests.

Holding the girl tight, I place my hands over her eyes, I hum to try to achieve the purest harmonic note possible. Close your eyes I said and don't open them till I say.

She closes her eyes. As I start to close mine, I see the faces of the community. They all blur into swirling colors.

Most are in shock. A few have envy. The Matriarchs are horrified. The community knows the Harmonics will never be the same again.

I feel myself reach a perfect note then move my harmonics to the extreme top of the spectrum. Hearing static, I know I am there.

Riveocea
Chapter 17

The Staircase

Sternly this time, I repeat, "Keep your eyes closed!"

Opening my eyes I see thousands of colorless heads shuffling in an endless stream. It worked. I made it to the Staircase without dying.

Tesla was right. The Static is just a note out of tune in the Harmonics.

Now can I get back? Focusing on my Harmonics, colors started swirling around me. I return to find us in a car heading out of town.

I see in the mirror the community gathering to watch us drive off. I sense they are filled with confusion and discord.

They were all upset. The Harmonics is in total confusion.

Taking my hands off her eyes, Sara is screaming, "What was that all about? How did we get here?"

Speaking as though I am her superior officer, "Need to know basis, and you don't need to know."

The 10 mile drive to the freeway was long and quiet. Sara did not say much. I felt the harmonics of the community diminish. By the time I reached the freeway, I could not hear the community at all.

We drove to the nearest restaurant to talk.

Sitting in the corner, so we can have some privacy, I scan the patrons. I see singular notes. Everyone playing their own tune, slightly off key. The older couple, in the opposite corner play a simplified two part harmony.

All I can think is, "Wow, Noobs; so lonely. I pity them all."

I start the conversation, "I'm sorry I had to get you out of there so quickly. You caused a great disturbance in the harmonics and we needed to leave before we…uh…. did any permanent damage."

She asks no questions but I need to somehow set things straight.

"About your report," I continue, "you have to understand that this society is special and our talents are unique."

"Got that right," Sara snorts.

"Please let me finish," I demand. "If you write the true report, HQ will send in more agents and you will lose them all to us. They will accept our way or be recycled. The harmonics is too dangerous for the world to handle. If the government even has a hint that it exists they will destroy us out of fear, then use it to control its citizens or even the rest of the world in the name of security. For all humanity sake you must not expose our town."

"But we already have your talents through technology." Sara responds, "We have wiretaps, satellites, and use through the wall technology, The CIA is even working on mind reading."

I point my finger at her, "It is not the same and you know it. Besides even those have all been abused. You have read my file.

"You know what I know. Can you deny it?

"Imagine the power of harmonics in the hands of a terrorist or any society that is ruled by fear. Even free societies would soon abuse the power. The temptation of control is just too great."

After a long silence Sara finally says, "I see your point."

I can sense her disbelief. She needs convincing. Making a gut decision I grab her hand. "Close your eyes again." She instinctively obeys.

With concentration I see colors start to move. Finding the static level, I stop.

The Staircase

We stand in silence for a moment. "Open your eyes," I command.

"What….Where are we? I don't understand."

No need for words, just look and take it in.

After several minutes, I explain, "We are at the top of the Harmonics. Anyone that is recycled ends up here forever. They can never escape.

"This would have been your fate.

"If society outside of Riveocea gets the power of the Harmonics they will start wars. Recycling all their enemies in the most horrendous wars of all time. Millions even billions will be trapped here for eternity.

"Do you want to be responsible for that?"

Sara starts to shiver uncontrollably. In a flood of tears she needs no words.

"Can I take you back now?"

"Please, Please," she cries.

Looking up at me as if I were her father, Sara finally says, "You're not coming back with me are you?"

I answer, "I am sending you back to the restaurant. I will not be with you. I am returning to where I belong. I have to go back and accept the consequence for my action."

"What if they recycle you?" she pleads.

Ignoring her plea, I say, "What are you going to do?"

"I'm going to write a report that says you were killed in the line of duty. A construction accident while undercover. You were trying to uncover a conspiracy that does not exist. The people of Riveocea are a harmless religious cult that does not appreciate outsiders and we are better off leaving them alone."

I breathe a sigh of relief, "Thank you."

"One last thing," she says, "If I change my mind, will they accept me back?

I smile inside and out, "absolutely."

In a blur of color she disappears. "She'll be back."

Riveocea
Chapter 20

I place myself at the 10 mile sign on the road to Riveocea. The walk home is long and agonizing but I have time to think. What am I going to tell them?

My thoughts keep rolling over in my head. My mind is a total conflicting mess.

Over 65 years passed since Hitler. How long will it take before the rest of the world is ready?

They will learn eventually. With my background in protecting civil rights and confronting abuses, I would be the perfect liaison to introduce them to harmonics.

The time will come when our secret will be out. But now is not the time. We must properly prepare them. I have seen the temptation. Will I be strong enough to keep them from going over the deep end?

Sara on the other hand may not be as strong. I know that. That is why, before I sent her back to the restaurant, I shot another untested bot.

In NTs' papers he described a memory bot that will apply

selective amnesia. I don't know if it works but if she starts spilling her guts to the government, hopefully, her memory of Riveocea will be erased.

After an hour of arguing inside my head I can see my path clearly. Now may not be the best time to introduce harmonics to the world, but when is the right time? Regardless of the outcome, I must face the music to bring the Harmonics back in tune.

My head is silent the rest of the walk. Filled with remorse and resignation, I leave my fate to the hands of the Matriarchs.

Riveocea
Chapter 21

As I make my way to the top of the hill I am filled with trepidation not knowing just what my reception will be after what I had done. Looking down on Riveocea I can feel the harmonics. The community waits for me in the center of town.

I relay my message of apology to the whole community. The matriarchs respond, "We already heard you, there was no need to repeat yourself."

Christ! I thought. I was so absorbed in self pity that I completely blinded myself from the harmonics. They sensed every thought!

The Matriarchs continue, "We understand now. It is we that must apologize to you. You prevented a terrible crime.

"You are more special than we ever could have imagined. Our arrogance prevented us from seeing another option. And sometimes that choice is NOT to live our way.

"Of course Sara is welcome back anytime and we have decided to retire the recycle-bot. It will never be used on humans."

Directly in front I hear a familiar voice, "Welcome home James."

Tess is waiting for me to come to her. I reach for her hands. She wraps her arms around me and tenderly kisses me on the lips. I close my eyes. Hearing the ring of a pure note, we see the pulsating rainbow of colors. Perfect harmonics.

The community joins in. Can this feeling ever be explained without experiencing it yourself? I doubt it. The community is back in harmony.

I cry silently to myself. Partially because of my happiness but also in sadness knowing what awaits our near future. The community feels it too.

"This is going to be a good life."

Staircase

Tess and I lived a full life in Riveocea. I went back into the Staircase after her death to look for her. Someday we will meet again.

It has been a while since Riveocea and I have no regrets. It may seem like Riveocea rescued me from a lifetime of despair. In reality it was only a fulcrum; the catalyst that expanded my mind to the possibilities.

Many would ask why anyone would enter the Staircase on purpose. When there are so many lost souls to help; How could I not? Hard to know where to start.

Doors seem to appear more frequently, as if extending me invitations. Now that I can come and go at will, it is my choice which doors I will enter.

You should hear the harmonics. They are everywhere. The static of the Staircase no longer drowns it out.

I have my work cut out for me. Drawing people away from the Staircase is not an easy thing.

So many are locked in the static. Lost in their thoughts, to them it may seem hopeless. I know how they feel. Few happy moments.

I can help here. There is always a way out. I can give them a light under a door to call them.

The possibilities are endless.

How was I to know that the Staircase was simply a stepping stone to understanding? Do I now understand what it is? No, not exactly. Some knowledge may be beyond comprehension.

Do I dread it or hate it? Not any more. It is simply life.

I need to teach them to stop avoiding the doors. Embrace life. Embrace fear, dreams, even the hurt.

Avoiding the inevitable is impossible. Life is a challenge that fills the harmonics with color. Our lives can be in tune or not. It is a choice.

Somehow, walking with the crowd actually has a pattern. The static has a tone in itself; a melody for me to follow and guide for my next move.

I hear it telling me to take the next door. I will use it to the full. Amazing how knowing the truth frees your spirit. Gazing at the massive number of heads bobbing in step, I see hope. The Stairway no longer controls me.

Almost on cue I pluck the perfect note and a new door appears. The sign says, "Girls, Girls, Girls".

I hold my breath, I wonder if it is possible…. Could Niki still be in there?"

I approach the door slowly and savor every moment. This time I am in control of what happens.

Not waiting for the door to automatically open, I turn the knob and swing the door open.

Portal 7

"Quantum levels in the life band is a reflection of who we are. Only in the absolute pitch of harmonics can we meet ourselves without creating a disturbance."

- The last works of JB -

Girls, Girls, Girls - 'De-Ja Vu'

Everything's the same.

Following the worn path on the wood floor, I make my way the bar stool. I spin the stool. It spins free, with no squeaks, because that is the way it should be.

Out of the corner of my eye I keep watch over the front door. It opens. A new customer enters the bar.

From the other end of the bar, the bartender winks at me. His image in the mirror behind him blurs slightly.

This time he pours my drinks without hesitation. No stall tactics. And oddly, he serves me first. Two drinks the bartender just poured are in front of me, waiting for my true love.

There she is. Walking toward me with a sultry, sexy confidence. She still makes my heart flutter.

Behind me I sense the hooded murderer poised with a knife.

As Niki gets closer, I can smell her familiar perfume. Her breath touches my face. When she starts to speak, I touch my finger to her beautiful lips and plead, "Don't say a word. Savor the moment."

I want time to stop. Staring deep into her eyes. I can see into her soul.

All this time she has been able to hear my tone. Now I can hear hers. Together our melody creates happiness throughout the harmonics.

I know more about her than I have ever known about anyone.

It is time to leave, but this time I will do it my way.

I hug her and say "Goodbye Niki." Stepping away from the bar, I abruptly storm for the front door. My heart is pumping.

The pressure in my eyes distort my vision. I feel a buzz from the drink I left on the bar. This time I didn't take the time to finish it. I didn't even take the time to talk.

Delay in the bar only has one outcome. This time it will be different.

As I reach the door to exit the bar, I hear movement behind me. Ignoring the urge to look, I briskly walk down the street.

Hearing foot steps behind me, I walk faster. Afraid to look, knowing the knife is headed for my back. I stop, close my eyes and ready myself for an exit to the staircase.

Niki's voice was soft and loving just like it always was. "I was wondering when you were going to finally get out of that hell hole."

I turn and stare at her with my mouth open, nothing coming out of it. I don't know what to say. I just stare.

Her coat is on. As her breathing slows I can see her breath in the cool midnight fog.

I have never seen her outside the bar. There is something magically different about her presence.

She touches my chin and gently closes my mouth. "You don't have to talk. Would you mind if I bought you a cup of coffee?"

Gathering my thoughts I finally say, "I would love it."

We talked for hours. The words flowed and I lost track of time. We talked about old times and new adventures. What we want in our futures and who we truly wanted to be. Something is different.

We walked the streets together as the sun peeked above the horizon and still no sign of the hooded killer. I don't know how long I have with my beautiful Niki but I am going to make the most of it.

I stop abruptly when I see the old hotel that I tried to get back to so many times before. Niki is facing me with her head down.

I start to speak as she whimsically tilts her head toward me. Her eyes and the corner of her mouth curl to make that all too familiar smile and says, "You know you can call me Tess."

"Yea I know."

Staircase
Epilogue

All the sad faces staring at their feet. The lost souls and unfulfilled lives. The mass of heads bobbing to a non-existent tune.

It is a huge undertaking to help all the lost souls in the harmonics. All I can do is take them down one note at a time. Even with three of us it may take an eternity.

I have plenty of time to reminisce meeting the woman of my dreams, at least twice. Or, who knows, maybe they all were my beloved Tess.

I haven't seen Tess since she went back into the Staircase but I am sure she is keeping herself busy trying to tune the Harmonics. There is much to do. My eternal soul mate and I have all the time in the universe to get it done.

I would treasure personally meeting Nikola Tesla, the man who started it all. I would thank him for guiding me, and let him know what a wonderful great grand daughter he has. Who knows, opportunities are endless here. Oh sure I saw him thrice, but he had on that hood and wielded a knife so it was not much of an introduction.

Every doorway has new potential. I don't remember seeing so many opportunities. I can't wait for my next adventure.

Another sign above a door reads, "Politician". Forget that one. I would have to kill myself too early.

Do I miss Tess? On the singular level, of course, but we work together as one and we have so many others to help. We both know where the door is. When she makes a call to me, I will be there with a simple note.

The sign over the next door says 'Bartender'.

Become a bartender? Why not! If someone needs a little nudge where else would they go?

Portal 8

"Fear is human, natural and frivolous. Fear not, for we are the Quantum Proctor."

- The last works of JB -

Bartender

Turning the knob, the door swings open without effort.

I find myself behind the bar. In the dark corner, Niki sits with a group at a table. She winks at me just as a salesman walks in the door. Glancing over my shoulder, I look at his image in the mirror. It blurs for an instant......

Without asking I start to pour his martini and smirk. He is gonna wait for this one; stirred not shaken.

54415539R00067

Made in the USA
Charleston, SC
01 April 2016